PUFFIN BO

Editor: Kaye

THE ADVENTURES OF UNCLE LUBIN

'I am going to be drowned after all,' said Uncle Lubin. 'I rather wish I had not come out today,' but that was the only time this good old man complained at all during the twelve amazing adventures he had in his search for his little lost nephew Peter.

Of course, it was his own fault that he'd gone to sleep while he was minding the baby, and let the horrid Bag-bird (which looked something like a stork) carry off the child, but no one but Uncle Lubin could have tried so hard and cheerfully to rescue the child, or been able to build an airship to travel to the moon, invent a submarine, defeat a dragon-snake by all-night concertina-playing, and conquer a hungry sea-serpent.

Uncle Lubin is one of the world's most unforgettable wandering heroes – a bit of an Odysseus, a bit of a Don Quixote, and crystallized for all time with the help of the author's marvellously funny and inventive illustrations. Seventy years after its first appearance, this classic story keeps all its old wit and sparkle, and lives on to delight a new generation of wonder-loving little boys and girls.

THE
ADVENTURES OF
UNCLE LUBIN

TOLD AND ILLUSTRATED
BY
W·HEATH·ROBINSON

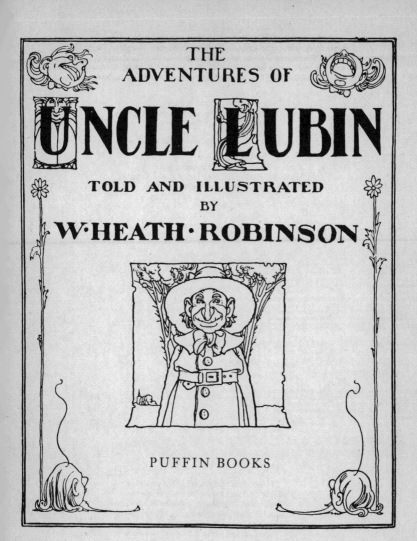

PUFFIN BOOKS

Puffin Books, Penguin Books Ltd, Harmondsworth, Middlesex, England
Penguin Books Inc., 7110 Ambassador Road, Baltimore, Maryland 21207, U.S.A.
Penguin Books Australia Ltd, Ringwood, Victoria, Australia
Penguin Books Canada Ltd, 41 Steelcase Road West, Markham, Ontario, Canada
Penguin Books (N.Z.) Ltd, 182-190 Wairau Road, Auckland 10, New Zealand

—

First published 1902
This edition published by the Minerva Press 1972
Published in Puffin Books 1975

This edition copyright © J. C. Heath Robinson and the Minerva Press Ltd, 1972

—

Made and printed in Great Britain by
Hazell Watson & Viney Ltd, Aylesbury, Bucks
Set in Monotype Caslon Old Face

DEDICATION

TO

E.M.R.

ENTLE INFANT,

For many years have I tried to find
some little person to whom I might dedicate
this book of wonderful stories; and of all
the small people I have ever met, you, I
think, will understand and love my old friend
Uncle Lubin.

Yes, for you, dear child, who nearly
always try to be perfect and often succeed;
you, who are so sorry for those in trouble,
and only sometimes cross when you are in
trouble yourself; you who hardly ever grizzle,

will, I am sure, admire Uncle Lubin, who was always so brave and good.

So, with the hope that you will not object, I respectfully dedicate this book to you; and when you know Uncle Lubin as well as I do, I am sure you will love him.

W. H. R.

CONTENTS

LIST OF ADVENTURES

List of Pictures

FIRST ADVENTURE

INTRODUCTION

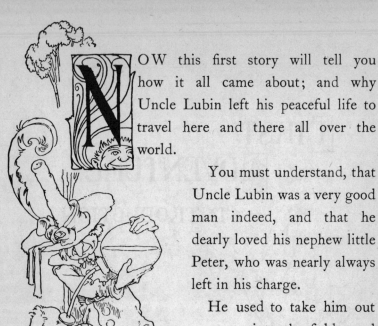

NOW this first story will tell you how it all came about; and why Uncle Lubin left his peaceful life to travel here and there all over the world.

You must understand, that Uncle Lubin was a very good man indeed, and that he dearly loved his nephew little Peter, who was nearly always left in his charge.

He used to take him out into the fields, and sing old songs to him; he used to gather flowers for him, and dance for him; sometimes he would tell him pretty stories to amuse him.

3

BUT one hot afternoon while Uncle Lubin was trying to sing little Peter to sleep, he himself fell asleep, quite unmindful of a wicked bag-bird which was watching in the branches overhead.

When the Bag-bird saw that Uncle Lubin was asleep, it stretched out
its long
neck
and snatched
little Peter
from
his
arms.

5

HEN little Peter began to make a great noise, and this woke Uncle Lubin, who saw with horror that his nephew was being carried off in the Bag-bird's beak. He was very frightened, too frightened to move in fact. Therefore he remained where he was. So the Bag-bird got clear away, and there was nobody to stop it.

6

HEN Uncle Lubin
got on to his feet
the Bag-bird was al-
ready flying over the
next field. 'I must
follow it,' said Uncle
Lubin, and he fol-
lowed it as fast as he could till
evening. Then he saw the
Bag-bird fly right up to
the moon, and he knew
that it would be
useless to run
after it any
more. And
he went
home,
feeling
very
down-hearted
indeed.

8

SECOND ADVENTURE
THE
AIR-SHIP

A LL next day the sorrowful Lubin racked his brain to find a way of rescuing little Peter. At last he decided to build an Air-ship, and he set about the work at once.

In a few days the ship was finished, and Uncle Lubin was able to start on his voyage.

Towards midnight he got quite near the moon, and found the wicked Bag-bird perched upon it.

N the other end of it he quickly

anchored

his

ship

and

climbed

up

the

side,

thinking

all

the

time

that

the

Bag-bird

had

not

seen

him.

15

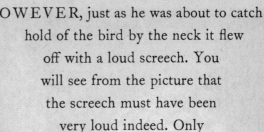

OWEVER, just as he was about to catch
hold of the bird by the neck it flew
off with a loud screech. You
will see from the picture that
the screech must have been
very loud indeed. Only
bag-birds can make
such screeches. And
when Uncle
Lubin heard
this
Bag-bird
screeching
he felt
sure
that
it
was
laughing
at
him.

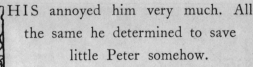

THIS annoyed him very much. All the same he determined to save little Peter somehow. So he crawled back to his air-ship. But, unfortunately, he found that the end of the moon had gone right through it and spoilt it entirely.

19

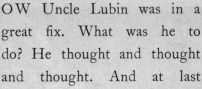

OW Uncle Lubin was in a great fix. What was he to do? He thought and thought and thought. And at last he said, 'I expect I shall have to jump.' Holding his hat firmly in his hands to prevent him from falling too quickly, he jumped right off the moon, and after a very long drop indeed he landed safely on the earth.

21

THIRD ADVENTURE

VAMMADOPPER

JUST look at the beautiful boat Uncle
Lubin built in order that
he might search the seas
for little Peter.
In this boat little Peter's
uncle sailed and
sailed for
many
months,
till
he
came
to
an
island
in
the
very
middle
of
the
sea.

24

 ERE he found a little old man
who was crying most bitterly.
'What is the matter
with you?' asked
Uncle Lubin
kindly. The
little
old
man
looked
at
him
through
his
tears
and
told
him
the
following
story:

Y name is Vammadopper, and many years ago, when I was quite young, I met a giant who was laughing. I said to him, 'Why do you laugh?' But he took no notice of me and went on laughing. I thought at first that he must be deaf.

29

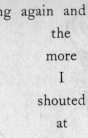S O I asked him why he kept on laughing again and again. But
the
more
I
shouted
at
him,
the
more
he
laughed,
till
at
last
I
could
bear
it
no
longer.

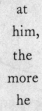

W.H.R.

 WAS so angry with him that I drew
my sword to fight him. But when
I rushed at him to make a
stroke he bent down,
and with a puff
blew me off
my feet as
though
I
were
a
feather.

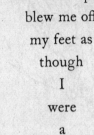

33

VER the clouds he blew me,
and over the mountains and
seas, till I dropped
on this island
where
I
have
remained
ever since.

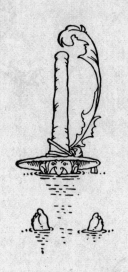

FOURTH ADVENTURE

THE CANDLE AND THE ICE-BERG

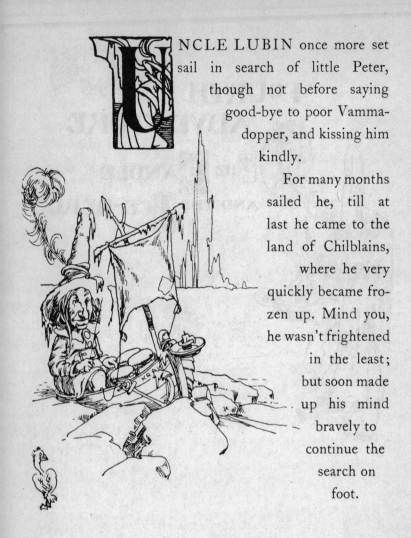

UNCLE LUBIN once more set sail in search of little Peter, though not before saying good-bye to poor Vamma-dopper, and kissing him kindly.

For many months sailed he, till at last he came to the land of Chilblains, where he very quickly became frozen up. Mind you, he wasn't frightened in the least; but soon made up his mind bravely to continue the search on foot.

NE evening, after tramping ever-so-many weary miles over the chilly ice-fields, Uncle Lubin heard the far-away note of the Bag-bird, teasing him and calling him names, from the top of an iceberg.

Lubin ran towards the berg, and as you see in the picture, he began to thaw it in two with the flame of his candle.

41

THE iceberg soon began to totter; and in a little while it fell. But sad to say it fell upon the poor head of Uncle Lubin; while the wicked Bag-bird, with screeches of joy, flew away into the night, still carrying little Peter in its beak.

43

FIFTH ADVENTURE

THE
SEA-SERPENT

POOR Uncle Lubin soon got over his disappointment and made up his mind to look for little Peter in the depths of the sea.

Therefore he built himself a wonderful boat which could keep under water for a long time and come up again all right.

When he had sailed in this boat many weeks he saw coming towards him a real sea-serpent.

 HEN Uncle Lubin at once
allowed his boat to sink,
while the hungry serpent
followed with mouth
wide open,
intending to
gobble him
right
up.

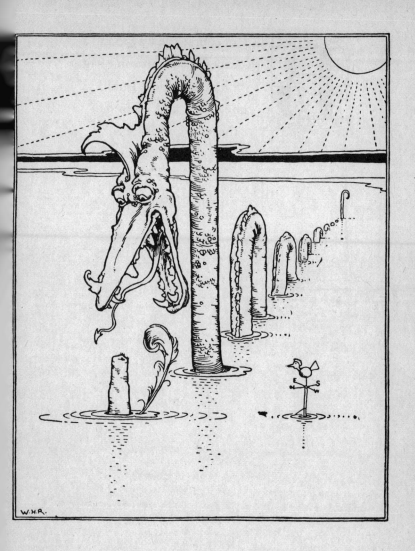

W.H.R.

49

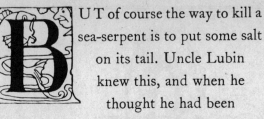

BUT of course the way to kill a
sea-serpent is to put some salt
on its tail. Uncle Lubin
knew this, and when he
thought he had been
long enough in the
water, he raised
his boat near
the
serpent's
tail,
and put
a
large
piece of
salt
on it.

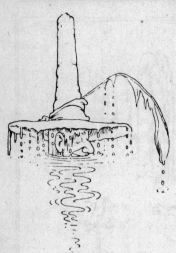

51

I NEED not tell you that this
caused the serpent great
pain, so much indeed
that he very
quickly
died,
and Uncle
Lubin
was
able to
go
on his
way
in
search
of
little
Peter.

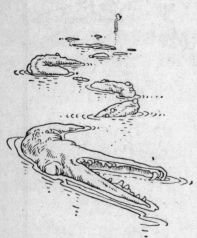

53

SIXTH ADVENTURE

The Mer-boy

ONE day while Uncle Lubin
was still sadly explor-
ing the depths of
the sea, he came
across a shoal
of little mer-
children.
One of the little
mer-boys caught
hold of the side of
Uncle Lubin's ship
and would not let go.
Uncle Lubin tried
to drive him off, but
in vain; so he brought
the little boy to
the surface of
the water.

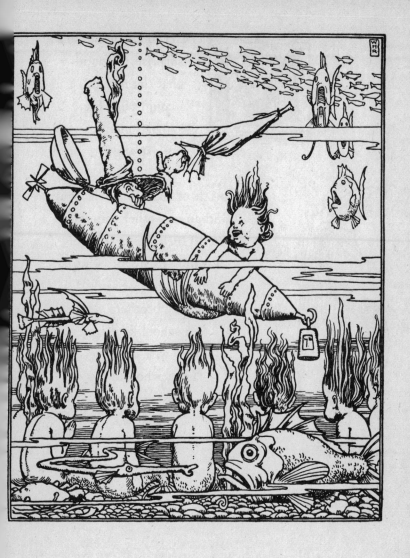

57

MUCH to Uncle Lubin's
surprise he found
that the mer-boy
could talk. He
had many
strange
tales
to tell of his life in the sea,
and among other things he
told Uncle Lubin the fol-
lowing sad story: 'Until
quite lately,' he said, 'I
and my brothers went
to a school kept by a
very wise old mer-
man, who did his
best to teach
us all we
ought to
know.'

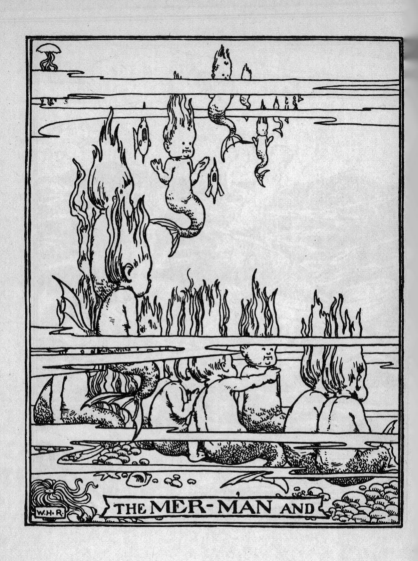

THE MER-MAN AND

THE HUMMING-TOP.

W.H.R.

NE afternoon he had been showing us how to spin a humming-top, and he was just beginning to explain to us why it hummed as it went round, when a great fish passing that way with its ugly mouth wide open, quietly swallowed the poor old mer-man right up.' 'What did you do?' asked Uncle Lubin. 'Well, we did nothing but laugh,' said the little mer-boy. 'That was not nice of you,' said Uncle Lubin.

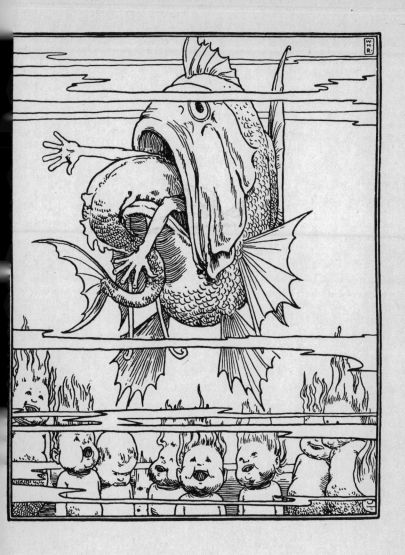

63

SEVENTH ADVENTURE
THE
BOY LUBIN

NCLE LUBIN was very much obliged to the little mer-boy for telling him such nice stories. And he said to him, 'I will now tell you a story. I remember that once when I was a little boy I got lost in a snowstorm. For many hours I wandered up and down trying to find my way home, but all in vain. At last I made up my mind that I had better spend the night in the snow, and I lay down by the side of what appeared to me to be a hat.

BUT I had scarcely
begun to doze off
when the hat seemed
to jump up of itself,
and out of the snow
there sprang a
funny little
old
man
who
looked
 for
all
the
world
like
a
Jack
in
the
Box.

HIS, of course, alarmed me. And I was more frightened still when the little old man brought out a large sword and said in terrible tones, "Now I will cut you to pieces." As I did not want to be cut to pieces, I ran away as fast as my legs could carry me, and without really knowing where I was going. As luck would have it, I ran straight to my home, and was able to sleep in bed that night after all.'

EIGHTH ADVENTURE

THE SHOWER

 NE afternoon, while Uncle
Lubin was out walking,
it began to rain. 'Dear
me,' he said, 'I
do believe it
is raining.'
And
he
ran
to
a
tree
for
shelter,
thinking
the
shower
would
soon
be
over.

THE rain came down very fast, however. Indeed, Uncle Lubin had never seen it rain so hard before, and he wondered if it was ever going to stop. Soon the whole of the country began to get flooded, and Lubin was obliged

to
climb
into
the
tree
to
prevent
himself
getting
drowned.

HE flood rose higher and higher all the afternoon, and at last it nearly covered the top of the tree. 'I am going to be drowned after all,' said Uncle Lubin. 'I rather wish I had not come out to-day.'

UT just as he was giving up all hope, he thought of a plan by which he might save his life. He had with him his old umbrella. 'I wonder if it would float,' he said. He turned it upside down and tried it. The old umbrella floated beautifully.

So Uncle Lubin
climbed
into
it and
sailed
away
on
his
travels.

81

NINTH ADVENTURE

THE CHARMING

OF THE

DRAGON-SNAKE

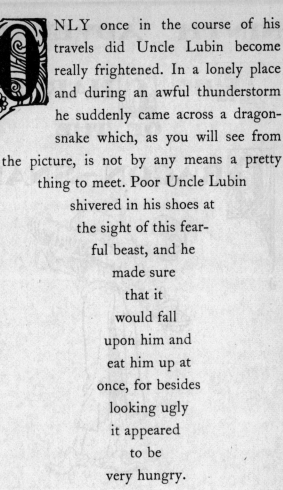

ONLY once in the course of his travels did Uncle Lubin become really frightened. In a lonely place and during an awful thunderstorm he suddenly came across a dragon-snake which, as you will see from the picture, is not by any means a pretty thing to meet. Poor Uncle Lubin shivered in his shoes at the sight of this fearful beast, and he made sure that it would fall upon him and eat him up at once, for besides looking ugly it appeared to be very hungry.

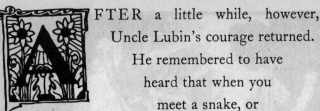

FTER a little while, however,
Uncle Lubin's courage returned.
He remembered to have
heard that when you
meet a snake, or
for that
matter
a dragon-snake,
the best
thing to
do is to
charm it
with music.
Fortunately Uncle
Lubin had
with him
his old
concertina. On
this he at once
began to play
some beautiful tunes.

THE dragon-snake was quite pleased with Uncle Lubin's playing and began to dance to it. Indeed, the snake danced and danced all night through, and by morning it had danced itself into such a tangle, and tied

itself into so many knots that it died. Playing the concertina all night tired Uncle Lubin very much, but he was quite glad to have saved his life once again.

TENTH ✻ ADVENTURE

THE DREAM.

B Y the side of the sea one evening
Uncle Lubin lay down to rest.
He took off his slippers and put
his head on a stone and fell fast
asleep. Soon he began to dream,
and his dreams were of little
Peter. He dreamed that the
fairies carried him through
the sky into one of the
most beautiful
meadows he
had ever
seen,
and
there
on
a beautiful throne

with a crown on his head and the
pretty flowers all round him, and two wise old men to
take care of him, sat little Peter, who had just been made
King of Fairyland. Uncle Lubin was ready to die with
joy at seeing his little nephew again.

UNCLE LUBIN'S DREAM

OF LITTLE PETER

N the shore Uncle Lubin slept
thus pleasantly dreaming for
several hours. Then he woke
up and knew that it was all a
dream. Oh how sad and lonely
and wretched he felt! And
when he thought of little
Peter and remembered
that he was still far
away from him
and perhaps
being badly
treated by
the cruel
Bag-bird,
the tears
rolled down
the old
man's
cheeks.

ELEVENTH ADVENTURE
THE
RAJAH.

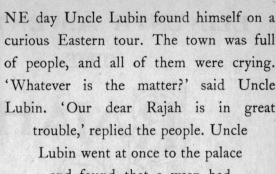

NE day Uncle Lubin found himself on a curious Eastern tour. The town was full of people, and all of them were crying. 'Whatever is the matter?' said Uncle Lubin. 'Our dear Rajah is in great trouble,' replied the people. Uncle Lubin went at once to the palace and found that a wasp had settled on the Rajah's nose, and was biting him as hard as ever it could. And nobody could persuade the wasp to go away.

101

103

D EAR, dear,' said Uncle Lubin, 'I will see to this.' So he had the Rajah taken into the courtyard and placed upon a mat. Then he aimed carefully at the wasp with his gun, and although the gun burst in his hands, it
made such
a great
noise
that
the
wasp
was
frightened
and
flew
away.

W.N.R.

105

TWELFTH ADVENTURE
THE
FINDING OF
LITTLE PETER

FTER all these journeys
and adventures Uncle
Lubin began to get rather
tired, and he almost gave
up hope of ever seeing
little Peter again. One
afternoon, however, he
happened to be walking
through a grove of palm-
trees. In the midst of his
walk he was disturbed by
a sudden shower of
cocoa-nuts which ap-
peared to be
thrown at
him from
the
tops
of
the
trees.

THE poor man was really upset by this. But he determined to find out who it was that could be so rude as to throw cocoa-nuts at him, and he therefore set to work to climb the tree from which the nuts had fallen.

III

LL that afternoon he climbed, and all night and all the next day. In fact he did not reach the top of the tree until he had climbed

two

nights

and

a

day.

So

that

the

tree

was

a

very

tall

one.

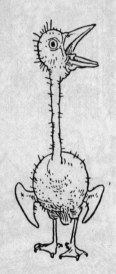

113

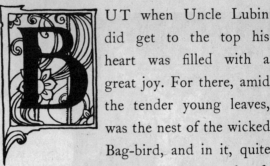

UT when Uncle Lubin did get to the top his heart was filled with a great joy. For there, amid the tender young leaves, was the nest of the wicked Bag-bird, and in it, quite warm and cosy and safe and sound among the little bag-chicks, was his dear nephew, little Peter. Of course Uncle Lubin kissed little Peter with all his might, and in a very few moments he had him out of the Bag-bird's nest and was running home with him as hard as ever he could. I am pleased to say that they got home quite safely and lived happily ever after.

115

THE ✻ END

Some other Young Puffins

DAVID AND HIS GRANDFATHER
Pamela Rogers

Three long stories about David and his kind, friendly Grandfather, who participates in all his secret schemes.

JACKO AND OTHER STORIES
Jean Sutcliffe

Stories about pets and people by an expert who is really in touch with young children – the creator of the *Listen With Mother* programme.

THE OWL WHO WAS AFRAID OF THE DARK
Jill Tomlinson

Being afraid of the dark has its problems, especially when you're a baby owl, but Plop comes to learn that the dark can be exciting, fun, beautiful and a lot else besides.

THE PENNY PONY
Barbara Willard

Life is never quite the same for Cathy and Roger after they find the penny pony in Mrs Boddy's shop.

FANTASTIC MR FOX

Roald Dahl

Every evening Mr Fox would creep down into the valley in the darkness and help himself to a nice plump chicken, duck or turkey, but there came a day when Farmers Boggis, Bunce and Bean determined to stop him whatever the cost . . .

PLAYTIME STORIES

Joyce Donoghue

Everyday children in everyday situations – these are stories for parents to read aloud and share with their children.

TALES OF JOE AND TIMOTHY
JOE AND TIMOTHY TOGETHER

Dorothy Edwards

Friendly, interesting stories about two small boys living in different flats in a tall, tall house, and the good times they have together. By the author of the *Naughty Little Sister* stories.

THE ANITA HEWETT ANIMAL STORY BOOK

A collection of cheerful, funny, varied animal stories from all over the world. Ideal for reading aloud to children of 5 or 6.

THE SHRINKING OF TREEHORN

Florence Parry Heide

'Nobody shrinks!' declared Treehorn's father, but Treehorn *was* shrinking, and it wasn't long before even the unshakeable adults had to admit it.

EMILY'S VOYAGE

Emma Smith

Emily Guinea-Pig leaves her cosy home to go on her first sea voyage – only to be shipwrecked on a tropical island with the crew of frightened rabbits and their lackadaisical captain.

CLEVER POLLY AND THE STUPID WOLF
POLLY AND THE WOLF AGAIN

Catherine Storr

Clever Polly manages to think of lots of good ideas to stop the stupid wolf from eating her.

BAD BOYS

ed. Eileen Colwell

Twelve splendid stories about naughty boys, by favourite authors like Helen Cresswell, Charlotte Hough, Barbara Softly and Ursula Moray Williams.

DUGGIE THE DIGGER AND HIS FRIENDS

Michael Prescott

As well as Duggie the Digger, there are tales about Horace the Helicopter, Bertram the Bus and Vernon the Vacuum Cleaner. It will please little boys who are interested in mechanical things.